# Contents

Chapter One

It was a crisp autumn day at
Oakwings Academy.

Poppy Merrymoss and her best
friends, Ninad Clearwater and Rose
Seedpip, were outside in gardening
class, listening carefully to their teacher,
Ms Mayblossom.

The forest was filled with colour -
oranges, browns, yellows and reds, as

the trees' leaves began changing. The ground was littered with crunchy fallen leaves and spiky conker shells.

"None of these leaves will go to waste," Ms Mayblossom was telling the class. "We collect as many as we can and put them on to the compost heap.

They mulch down as they rot away and we use that mulch to help the new seeds and plants grow."

Ninad's pet ladybird, Spot, who had been perched on his shoulder, opened his wings and flew down to the ground. He began rolling around in the leaves.

Poppy laughed at him. "That looks like fun!"

Rose giggled and picked up an armful of leaves then threw them up into the air. They twisted and spun as they floated down to the ground.

Ms Mayblossom, who was also Poppy's aunt, cleared her throat and

gave Poppy and Rose a pointed look.
"As I was saying, I have invited a
special guest along to our gardening
class today to talk to you about leaf
mould."

Poppy scrunched up her nose. "Leaf
mould? That doesn't sound much fun,"
she muttered.

"Oh no! It gets worse," Rose
whispered. "Look who the special guest
is!"

Ms Webcap came flying over, landing
in front of the class.

The friends groaned as Ms Webcap
smirked at them.

"What's she doing here?" Ninad
hissed.

Ms Webcap was deputy head at
Oakwings Academy. Poppy and her
friends had recently discovered that she
was also the evil Lady Nightshade. But
only Poppy, Rose and Ninad knew
of her true identity. They had tried to
tell the grown-up fairies, but nobody
believed them.

"Probably up to no good as usual,"
Rose replied.

"Gather around, class," Ms Webcap
called. She held out a handful of
crumbling leaves. "These dead leaves

might look useless to you, but the mould they turn into is wonderful for our forest, helping the plants and flowers grow."

Poppy glanced at Rose, her eyebrows raised.

At the front of the class, Poppy and Rose's roommate, Celeste, crinkled her nose. "Why does it smell so bad?" she asked. "Mould is disgusting!"

As the rest of the class giggled, Ms Webcap's face turned an angry shade of red. She glared at Celeste for a moment, before turning to Ms Mayblossom. "I've just remembered I have something urgent to deal with," she said, storming off before Ms Mayblossom could say a word.

"Oh," Ms Mayblossom said, watching her go. "In that case, class, I have an air spell to teach you."

She pointed her wand at a pile of leaves and made a circle in the air. "Whisk up, whoosh up, wind up!" she sang.

The leaves stirred then lifted from the ground, swirling in spirals in the air. Ms Mayblossom pointed her wand at a giant empty tub, on the ground nearby, which was made from woven willow. The leaves flew inside, settling into a messy pile.

"Wow!" Rose said. "Do you think that would work with the dirty laundry in our bedroom?"

Poppy giggled.

"Now, we add water," Ms Mayblossom told them. This time, she pointed her wand at a puddle nearby. "Let's do the raindrop spell!" she sang.

Large droplets of water rose from the puddle and into her wand. Ms Mayblossom swished her wand at the tub and the droplets gently rained down into it, soaking the leaves.

"Now it's your turn," she told the class. "Try to gather as many leaves as you can into the tub, then add water."

"Whisk up, whoosh up, wind up!"
Poppy cried.

She smiled delightedly as the leaves
swirled into the air. She managed to
get most of them into the tub.

Rose tried the spell next. "Whisk up,
whoosh up, wind up!" A few leaves
accidentally flew in the opposite
direction, but most of them landed in
the tub. "I did it!" she said proudly.

"You should do the water spell,
Ninad," Poppy said.

"You're so good at water magic!"
Rose agreed.

"Drip and drop!" Ninad cried, with a huge grin on his face.

As usual he had no trouble at all with the water spell. The droplets rained down on to the leaves in the tub.

"I like doing water spells," Ninad said. "But I really want to become a water animal fairy."

There were many different types of fairies, but the young fairies wouldn't discover what kind they would become until they finished their training at Oakwings. The type of wands they had sometimes gave them a clue though. Ninad had a willow wand, usually the type of wand water fairies had.

Ms Mayblossom gathered the class together.

"In a year's time, the leaves and water will have turned into mulch," she said, "which, as Ms Webcap told you, becomes leaf mould to help the flowers and plants grow."

"A year is a loooong time to wait!" Rose groaned. "Isn't there a magic spell we can use to make it grow quicker?"

Ms Mayblossom was about to answer
when the sky turned dark overhead.

Poppy grabbed Rose's arm. "It's Lady
Nightshade! Look!"

Lady Nightshade
hovered in the
air above. Her
long black
cloak was
made from
dead leaves,
and her skirt
was covered
in silver

cobwebs. Her pet spider, Webby, sat on top of her head like a hat.

Unlike the other types of fairies who used wands, Lady Nightshade used fungus to cast her spells. She held her magic toadstool high in the air and shot bolts of fizzing black magic at the giant tub filled with leaves.

Then she uttered a spell:

"Fallen leaves turn into mould,
Spread through this forest, like a cold.
Do not mock my deadly power,
Some plants you don't want to flower!"

In a flash, the leaves in the tub began crumbling. They turned brown, then a slimy green colour as they transformed into mould. Spurts of the greeny-brown mould shot out of the tubs spreading through the air and out into the forest.

Rose frowned. "Did Lady Nightshade just do a spell to help us grow the mould faster?"

"Surely she hasn't turned good?" Ninad said.

Poppy shivered with dread and shook her head. "I'm not sure," she said, feeling confused. "But Lady Nightshade doesn't usually do anything to help others."

Chapter Two

Poppy woke with a start to the sound of Celeste screaming at the top of her lungs. On the top bunk, above Poppy, Rose's wings flung open in surprise and she tumbled on to the floor.

"What's going on?" Rose squealed, rubbing her bottom.

Poppy jumped out of bed to help Rose up. "Are you OK?"

"Never mind *Rose*!" Celeste squealed. "What about *me*? I'm trapped!"

Poppy turned to look at Celeste and her eyes widened. Twisty, winding weeds had crept into the open bedroom window during the night and Celeste's bed . . . and Celeste . . . were covered in them.

"They are trying to get me and turn me into mulch!" Celeste cried. She flapped her wings wildly and thrashed her legs until she was free from the weeds. Then she flew to the other side of the room.

Poppy and Rose followed the trail of vines to the window and looked outside.

"Oh no!" Poppy gasped. "There is knotweed everywhere!"

Long, thin stems bearing large green leaves had crept up the sides of the old oak tree, as though they were trying to swallow it whole. Some of the teachers, including Ms Mayblossom, were outside using spells to try to cut the knotweed back.

"How did it grow so quickly?" Rose asked.

Poppy's stomach sank as she realised what had happened. "Lady Nightshade's spell!" she cried. "She wasn't trying to help the plants grow. She wanted the powerful leaf mould to make the knotweed grow!"

Celeste leaned out of the window to take a look. "It's not just Oakwings Academy it has taken over," she said, with trembling wings. "It's the whole of

the forest!" She sniffed the air. "It's so stinky!" Avoiding the trails of knotweed, she flounced over to her bedside table and pulled out a tiny crystal bottle of perfume. Then she sprayed it over herself, until the whole room was filled with a flowery-smelling cloud.

Rose's eyes began to water as she sneezed.

"That's better!" Celeste said, taking a deep breath. She showed Poppy and Rose the bottle. "This is made from the finest magnolia petals, collected by a special breed of rare pink mice," she told them. "They use their tiny paws to mix it with early morning dew."

Rose sneezed again, then grinned. "It's a bit like leaf mould then," she said. "Your perfume is magnolia mulch."

Poppy covered her face to stop herself from laughing.

Celeste scowled, then threw on a dress and stormed out of the bedroom, leaving a trail of flowery perfume behind her.

After they got dressed, Poppy and Rose went down to the Great Hall for breakfast. The hall was usually full of noise and excitement about the day

ahead. But this morning, it was quiet. Fairies spoke in hushed voices and the teachers all had worried looks on their faces.

When they were all seated, the headmistress, Madame Brightglow, flew to the front of the hall. She was a sunshine fairy and always looked to be glowing and happy, but today she looked more serious than Poppy had ever seen her. Everyone fell silent as she spoke.

"Fairies," she began, "our forest is facing an emergency. As you will all know by now, Lady Nightshade put a spell on the leaf mould to make the knotweed grow impossibly fast. We are trying to remove it, but each time we do, more knotweed grows back in its place. I'm afraid that if it continues to grow like this, it will kill all of the plants and flowers in the forest."

There were gasps and cries around the Great Hall. The fairies and all of the animals who lived in the forest wouldn't survive if the plants and trees died.

Poppy grabbed hold of Rose's hand and blinked back tears.

"We are going to need every single

fairy's help to fight this knotweed," Madame Brightglow said.

Another teacher joined Madame Brightglow at the front of the hall. It was Mr Mossmead, who was an air fairy. He wore a green suit made from moss, with apple seed buttons down the front of his jacket.

"First years!" he called. "You are to come with me."

Poppy, Rose, Ninad and the rest of their class followed Mr Mossmead from the hall and outside.

Ninad's eyes grew wide at the sight of all the knotweed. It twisted up and around the tree trunks and across the ground, making tangled bushes. The whole forest was covered. "I knew it was bad," he said, "but I didn't think it was this bad."

"I am going to show you a spell to help pull up the knotweed," Mr Mossmead told them. "Pay close attention to the words."

He recited an air spell:

"Pluck and pull, drag and haul, yank them all!"

When he pointed his wand at a patch of knotweed, the air seemed to suck the weeds out of the ground, bit by bit, until the ground was clear again.

Poppy clapped, feeling relieved that at least there was something they could do to help. She still didn't know what type of fairy she was going to become, and she had an oak wand which could be used by many different types of fairies. But her dad was an air fairy, and she knew she could do air spells well.

"Go off into the forest in groups of three and get to work," Mr Mossmead said.

Poppy, Rose and Ninad set off into the forest, finding a particularly large clump of knotweed, and set to work.

"Pluck and pull, drag and haul, yank them all!" Poppy shouted.

The spell worked, and although she pulled out fewer weeds than Mr Mossmead had done, she was still pleased with her progress. Ninad and Rose were having slightly more trouble.

Ninad could only pull out one or two weeds at a time.

"Pluck and pull, drag and haul, yank them all!" Rose yelled excitedly. She swished her wand towards the weeds so hard that it flew out of her hand and she flew backwards, knocking Celeste to the ground.

"Rose!" Celeste shrieked. "Why are you so clumsy all the time?"

"Sorry," Rose mumbled. "It was an accident."

Celeste got to her feet and brushed down her rose petal dress. "Come on!" she ordered her teammates. "Let's find

somewhere less dangerous!" They flew away through the forest.

Poppy, Rose and Ninad continued the spell, slowly clearing a patch of ground.

"I knew Lady Nightshade was up to no good when she did that mould spell!" Rose huffed.

"I wish the teachers would listen to us," Poppy said. "If they knew the truth about Ms Webcap being Lady Nightshade, we could get her far, far away from our forest and no bad things would happen."

Ninad frowned. "There's one thing

I don't understand," he said. "Lady Nightshade said *some plants you don't want to flower.*" He pointed to the knotweed. "The knotweed doesn't have any flowers. What do you think she meant?"

Rose opened her mouth to say something, then paused and sniffed the air. She glanced down at Spot, who had been dozing close by.

"Eww, Ninad. Your pet ladybird is a bit stinky."

Ninad glared at Rose. "Spot is very clean, thank you very much!"

Poppy frowned. "Rose is right,

though. What is that awful smell?"

They breathed in, following the smell through the forest as it got stronger and stronger until they came to a big tangle of weeds.

Rose pinched her nose. "It's worse than Celeste's perfume!" she groaned.

Poppy knelt down and examined the weeds.

"Be careful," Ninad said. "It could be another one of Lady Nightshade's horrible spells."

"I think there's something under here," Poppy said. She pulled at the knotweed and saw a patch of red fluffy fur.

Ninad and Rose helped pull away the rest of the weeds, and Poppy gasped.

"It's a red panda!" Ninad exclaimed.

Chapter Three

The red panda trembled as he looked up at the fairies with his big black eyes.

"He's scared!" Ninad said, reaching forward to pat the red panda's head.

That seemed to calm the red panda down a little. He leaned into Ninad's hand with a small smile.

"We won't hurt you," Poppy said.

The little red panda was super cute.

He had crimson fur and a stripy tail
which was as long as his body. Poppy
stroked his head and his smile grew. His
fur felt soft and warm, and his face was
white with red marks below his eyes,
which looked like tears.

"I think he's just a baby," Ninad said.

"Are you lost?" Poppy asked the red panda. "I've never seen a red panda in the forest before."

The red panda nodded his head. "Meat here," he snuffled.

Poppy frowned and looked to Ninad and Rose. They both seemed as confused as she was.

"There is no meat here," Poppy told the red panda gently.

"Maybe he's hungry?" suggested Rose.

Ninad shook his head. "I don't think red pandas eat meat." He stroked the red panda softly. "Don't worry, little one, we'll find you some food."

"What's your name?" Rose asked.

"Meat here," the red panda replied. "Boo-boo, flower die, whisper water!"

"I'm sorry," Poppy said. "We don't understand."

The red panda shook his head and bunched up his small paws. "Boo-boo, flower die, whisper water!" he repeated, looking more and more upset.

"I think he's trying to tell us that something bad has happened," Ninad said.

"Maybe he was trying to find help

when he got caught up in the weeds?"
Rose suggested.

Poppy scratched her head. "This is
harder to work out than one of Lady
Nightshade's curses!"

Rose and Poppy gently stroked the
red panda's fur again to calm him
down.

"Did you know that red pandas are
excellent at climbing trees?" Ninad
told them. He pointed to the red
panda's tear-shaped patches on his face.
"And those patches on his face help
to protect his eyes from the sunlight.
They also use their long tails to keep

themselves warm when it gets chilly and they lick their fur to stay clean."

Poppy raised her eyebrows, impressed at Ninad's knowledge.

"How do you know so much about red pandas?" she asked.

Ninad shrugged. "I love all animals," he said. "And I've been learning about all kinds of animals for when I become a water animal fairy. Did you know that red pandas can let off a horrible smell to scare predators away when they're afraid?"

"So *that's* what that terrible smell was!" Rose gasped. "I wish I had

that ability. I'd love to get revenge on Celeste when she sprays her stinky perfume all around our bedroom!"

Poppy laughed. "I don't think your red panda smell would be much better!"

Ninad's smile faded. "How do you think he got here?" he asked. "Why is he all alone? And why is he asking for meat?"

"Meat here!" the red panda snuffled sadly.

Poppy sighed. "What are we going to do?" she said. "It's getting late and we can't leave him here all by himself.

Especially not with all of this knotweed. He'll get himself stuck again."

"He'll have to come back to Oakwings with us," Rose said. "We have got a spare bed in our room after all."

Poppy thought about it for a moment. Animals weren't allowed in the bedrooms at Oakwings. But the red panda was only young, and she couldn't bear to think of him out in the forest all alone at night.

The little red panda shivered. He wrapped his long fluffy tail around himself like a blanket to keep warm.

"Come with us," Poppy said. "We will look after you."

They led him through the forest until they came to Oakwings Academy. The fairies had done a good job of clearing the knotweed from the oak tree.

Rose flew ahead to make sure nobody was around, then Poppy and Ninad hurried the red panda up the twisty stairs to Rose and Poppy's room.

"We're going to be in so much

trouble if anyone finds out," Ninad whispered, glancing around nervously.

"We can't leave him outside alone," Poppy said.

Ninad nodded. "Quick, before anyone sees us."

Rose opened the door slowly and peeped her head around it to see if Celeste was inside. She nodded to Poppy to let her know the room was empty and they quickly bundled the red panda inside, on to the spare bed.

"You'll be safe here," Poppy told the red panda. "Tomorrow we will try to find your family."

There was the sound of footsteps and flapping wings outside, then a loud knocking on the door.

"Celeste is coming!" Ninad hissed from outside.

"We need to hide him!" Poppy cried.

Rose quickly threw a blanket over the red panda, then Poppy and Rose flew on to their beds and pretended to look busy.

"Ugh!" Celeste huffed loudly as she came into the room. "I am sooooo exhausted from doing spells on all that disgusting knotweed."

She threw her bag on to the spare

bed, right on top of where the red panda was hiding. Rose's eyes grew wide and Poppy held her breath as she waited for the red panda to move or make a noise. Luckily, he stayed quiet. But then something even more worrying happened.

Celeste sniffed at the air, then spun round to glare at Rose and Poppy.

"What is that disgusting smell!" she shrieked, flapping one hand in front of her face and pinching her nose with the other.

Rose and Poppy glanced at each other.

"It's . . . um . . . it's my new perfume," Rose blurted out.

Poppy smothered a laugh as Celeste continued to waft the air around her.

"Perfume?!" Celeste gagged. "What is it made from? Stale pond water mixed by stinky skunks?"

She quickly grabbed her perfume and sprayed huge clouds of it around the room until Rose and Poppy began coughing and spluttering. Then she jumped into her bed and pulled the covers over her head. In no time, she was snoring loudly.

Poppy let out a big sigh of relief. Their room might smell disgusting but at least Celeste hadn't discovered their new roommate!

Chapter Four

The next morning, Poppy, Rose and Ninad snuck the red panda out of Oakwings Academy early, so they wouldn't be spotted.

They had almost been caught by Ms Mayblossom, but Poppy had told her that they were so worried about the knotweed they wanted to get an early start.

They hurried through the forest to the place where they had discovered the red panda.

"Maybe we'll find some clues about where he came from?" Poppy wondered out loud as they set about clearing away the knotweed.

"If only he could tell us why he's here or where he came from," Rose said.

"Meat here," the little red panda yelped. "Boo-boo, flower die, whisper water!"

"He keeps on saying that," Ninad said. "I wish we could figure out what it means."

Poppy finished pulling up the last of the knotweed, then wiped her forehead. There were no clues to be seen.

"Let's ask some of the animals in the forest," she suggested. "One of them might know the red panda or might have seen where he came from."

Ninad nodded. "Good idea."

They set off through the trees, the fallen leaves crunching under their feet. Finally, they found themselves at the river.

The red panda sipped the water, then wiped his mouth with the back of his paw. "Whisper water," he said.

On the other side of the river, a beaver was collecting fallen sticks to use to build a dam.

"Excuse me!" Ninad called out.

The beaver looked up and smiled at the fairies. He put down his wood and swam across the river to them.

"Hello!" the beaver said cheerfully.

"Hello," Ninad, Rose and Poppy replied in unison.

Ninad pointed to the little red panda. "We were wondering if you knew this red panda. We think he's lost and we are trying to find his family."

The beaver clasped his front paws and studied the red panda. "Hmmm, I don't think I've seen a red panda in the forest before," he grunted. "Maybe he comes from somewhere else?"

Poppy sighed. "That's what we thought."

"Boo-boo, flower die, whisper water," the red panda said.

The beaver frowned. "What does that mean?"

"We were hoping you might know," Rose replied.

The beaver studied the red panda again. "Maybe he's saying he is sad that the flowers die, and the water is talking to him?" he suggested.

Poppy narrowed her eyes. "Maybe," she said slowly. She turned to Ninad and Rose. "And maybe we should ask someone else?"

Her friends nodded and said goodbye to the beaver then continued on through the forest.

There was a rustle in a pile of leaves up ahead. The friends stopped as a hedgehog poked his head out.

"Hullo!" the hedgehog squeaked.

"Hello," the friends said, waving at the hedgehog.

"Have you seen all of the knotweed?" the hedgehog asked. "It's terrible, terrible!" he muttered as he continued sniffling

through the leaves.

"Have you ever seen a red panda before?" Poppy asked.

The hedgehog shook his head. "What's a red panda?"

Ninad pointed to the red panda.

"Ahh," the hedgehog said. "Nice to meet you."

"Boo-boo, flower die," the red panda replied.

"We don't know what he's trying to tell us," Poppy explained. "We're trying to find his family."

"He might be trying to scare you," said the hedgehog. "Boo!" he shouted

loudly, causing the little red panda to jump in fright.

Poppy frowned. "I don't think so. Besides, he's too cute and fluffy to be scary."

They left the hedgehog to his pile of leaves and set off in another direction. Here, the trees grew tall and the floor was covered in pine needles.

There was a loud *HOOT!* overhead and Poppy looked up to see a wise old owl sitting high up in the branches of a pine tree.

"Owls know everything!" Poppy said. "Let's go and ask her if she knows where the red panda came from."

"I'll stay here with the red panda,"
Ninad said.

Rose and Poppy flew up to the high
branches of the tree and landed beside
the owl. She had her eyes closed, but
her head swivelled slightly towards
them.

"Whooooo are youuuuu?" the owl
asked.

She had snowy white feathers and
her long, sharp talons gripped the
branch.

Poppy gulped. "I'm Poppy and this
is Rose, and we wanted to ask you a

question, wise owl."

The owl nodded. "Ask away."

"It's about the red panda down below," Poppy told her. "We found him

alone in the woods. He keeps on saying 'boo-boo, flower die, whisper water'. Do you know what that might mean?"

The owl opened one eye and peered down at Ninad and the red panda on the ground far below.

"He probably means *bambooooooo*," the owl hooted.

"Red pandas eat bamboo and live in bamboo forests."

"That's it!" Poppy cried. "Do you know where the bamboo forest is?"

The owl shook her head. "No, I like to stay close to my tree."

"What about Dr Littlewing?" Poppy said to Rose. Dr Littlewing looked after the animals in the sanctuary at Oakwings. "She has a bamboo wand, and she knows all about different types of animals."

"Maybe she'll know where the bamboo wands are from," Rose said. Her wings fluttered excitedly.

"Thank you, wise owl!" Poppy flew off the tree branch and beckoned to Rose. "Come on. Let's go back to school and ask her."

Chapter Five

They found Dr Littlewing in the animal sanctuary at Oakwings. The sanctuary was lined with pens, boxes and beds, all containing different creatures who needed help.

They passed by a box filled with hanging chrysalises, which wriggled back and forth as though the butterflies inside were about to burst out. A little

further along was a bed filled with tiny
newborn guinea pigs. Ninad leaned
over to tickle them and they squeaked
excitedly.

"I think they like you, Ninad," Dr
Littlewing said, coming to join them.

"They're so cute!" Rose cooed.

"We need your help, Dr Littlewing," Poppy said. She moved to the side to reveal the red panda who had been hiding behind them.

Dr Littlewing gasped. "I haven't seen a red panda for a long time."

"We found him caught up in the knotweed in the forest," Poppy explained. "But we don't know where he's come from or what his name is. All he keeps saying is boo-boo, flower die, whisper water."

Rose nodded. "An owl helped us work out that boo-boo means bamboo, because it's what red pandas eat."

"And they live in the bamboo forest," Ninad added.

"So we thought that as you are an animal fairy and have a bamboo wand, you might know where the bamboo . . . and the red panda come from?" Poppy finished.

Dr Littlewing flew over to the red panda and examined him. "He's very young," she said. "But he seems to be in good health."

She flew over to a box and pulled a bamboo shoot from it, then flew back to hand it to the red panda, who began happily munching on it.

"Poor thing," Ninad said. "He must have been so hungry!"

"We thought he wanted to eat meat," Poppy told Dr Littlewing. "He keeps saying 'meat here'."

"Hmm, very strange," Dr Littlewing replied. "Red pandas don't eat meat. There is a bamboo forest between the Snowflake Mountains and the Whispering Waterfall. Maybe that's where he came from?"

"Whisper water!" The friends exclaimed.

"That must be what he meant," Rose said.

Poppy grinned. "So now we know that boo-boo means bamboo and whisper water is the Whispering Waterfall. He was trying to tell us where he came from."

Rose crinkled her nose. "What about meat here, though, and flower die?"

Poppy put her hands on her hips. "There's only one way to find out," she said. "We are going to have to go to the bamboo forest."

They thanked Dr Littlewing and took a few more bamboo shoots for the red panda, then headed out of the animal sanctuary.

Just as they turned towards the forest, they heard the buzz of wings close by.

"Someone's coming!" Ninad hissed.

Poppy peeped out from behind a tree to see who it was. "It's Ms Webcap! We need to hide the red panda."

They hid the red panda behind a bush and returned to the path just in time to see Ms Webcap flying straight towards them.

She landed in front of them with a smug look on her face. "Just where do you think you three are off to in such a hurry?" she asked.

"We're going to pull up more

knotweed, Ms Webcap," Poppy said, smiling sweetly.

Ms Webcap narrowed her eyes at each of the young fairies in turn. "I'll be watching you three," she said, menacingly. Then she flew off in the direction of the animal sanctuary.

When they were sure she was gone, they fetched the red panda from the bush. He was still munching happily on the bamboo.

"Let's go and find your family," Poppy told him.

The red panda smiled. "Whisper water?" he asked.

Poppy nodded. "That's right. We're going to the Whispering Waterfall."

They set off through the forest, in the direction of the mountains. When they got there, Ninad pointed up ahead.

"Look at that!" he said.

A rush of water cascaded down between two of the mountains, making a *shhhhhhh* sound.

"That must be the Whispering Waterfall," Rose said.

The red panda saw the waterfall and began bouncing up and down.

"Boo-boo!" he cried. "Whisper water!"

He scampered off ahead on all four paws and the fairies flew after him.

"He's really fast for a baby!" Poppy puffed.

Finally, the red panda stopped at the edge of another forest. Tall bamboo stalks of blue and green reached up high into the air. They were covered in pretty pink, red and white flowers, and they gently waved back and forth in the light breeze.

"It's beautiful!" Rose gasped.

"This must be why he kept on saying flower," Poppy said. "He was talking about the bamboo."

"But why did he say die?" Ninad asked.

They looked at the red panda, who stared sadly at the ground.

There was a rustle in the bamboo, and another, larger red panda emerged through the stalks. She was followed by three tiny red panda babies.

"You're home!" she cried, rushing to

hug the red panda. He smiled happily
as the tiny pandas joined the hug. Then
the larger red panda noticed the fairies.

"Hello!" she said. "I'm Mrs Fluffytail."

Poppy, Ninad and Rose introduced themselves and told Mrs Fluffytail all about how they had found the little red panda tangled in knotweed and how they had used his clues to find their way back to her.

"Thank you!" Mrs Fluffytail said. "I had to send my eldest son, Tear, to try to get help. I couldn't leave the babies and they're too small to travel."

Rose blinked at Mrs Fluffytail, then at the small red panda. "He's called Tear?"

"Yes," Mrs Fluffytail nodded. "After

the tear-shaped patches on his face."

Ninad and Poppy burst out laughing.

"He wasn't saying *meat here*!" Ninad spluttered. "He was saying *me, Tear*. He was trying to tell us his name!"

Poppy and Rose giggled and stroked Tear's fur. The tiny baby red pandas nuzzled up to the fairies, their fur tickling their faces.

"We've finally solved the riddle of the red panda," Poppy exclaimed. She was so happy to see Tear back with his family.

"But why did Tear keep saying *die*?" Rose asked.

Mrs Fluffytail's tail drooped sadly.

"Once the bamboo flowers, it means it is going to die," she told them. "If all of the bamboo trees in the forest flower at the same time, it means they will all die at the same time."

"Oh no!" Ninad gasped. "Then the red pandas will have no food!"

Mrs Fluffytail nodded. "That is why I had to send Tear for help. We can't let the bamboo die. We won't survive without it."

Poppy's stomach churned. "That's what Lady Nightshade meant in her curse when she said *some plants you*

don't want to flower. Bamboo is a plant you don't want to see flower because it means it is going to die!"

"Her extra-powerful mulch made the knotweed *and* the bamboo grow faster!" Ninad said. "The red pandas won't have anything to eat."

Poppy clenched her fists. She was so angry at Lady Nightshade. They had to do something!

"It's not all terrible," Mrs Fluffytail told them. "The bamboo flowers contain seeds. We can gather and plant them to grow new bamboo."

Poppy breathed a sigh of relief. "We'll

help you plant them!"

Ninad and Rose nodded eagerly. But before they could get to work, the sky above darkened. A loud, evil cackle echoed around them as the air turned cold. Hovering above them with a wicked gleam in her eyes was Lady Nightshade.

Chapter Six

Poppy and her friends looked on in horror as bolts of black magic shot out of Lady Nightshade's magic toadstool. Puffs of greeny-black mould floated in clouds around them. Poppy held her nose as a foul smell filled the air and watched, helpless, as more of the powerful leaf mould spread through the bamboo forest.

"You'll never stop me, you stupid little
fairies!" Lady Nightshade shrieked.
"Fungus magic is the most powerful of
all!"

More and more flowers sprung up on the bamboo stalks as the leaf mould worked its magic. Lady Nightshade's pet spider, Webby, bounced up and down happily on her head and poked his tongue out at the fairies.

"She's making the bamboo die even quicker!" Rose cried.

"We have to stop her!" Poppy said.

She glanced around, trying to think of anything that they could use to stop Lady Nightshade. Just beyond the edge of the bamboo, the ever-growing knotweed was creeping its way further across the fairy forest.

"The knotweed!" Poppy whispered.
"We can use our magic to pull it out of
the ground and tie her up."

Rose grinned. "That's brilliant!" she
whispered back.

"We could tangle her up just like
poor Tear was tangled," Ninad agreed.

Poppy, Ninad and Rose pointed
their wands at the knotweed. "Pluck
and pull, drag and haul, yank them
all," they chanted quietly so Lady
Nightshade wouldn't hear them. "Pluck
and pull, drag and haul, yank them
all!"

While Lady Nightshade continued

to use her magic toadstool to spread
the leaf mould, the friends pulled up
long vines of knotweed. When they
had enough, they flew around Lady
Nightshade in circles, using air magic
to bring the knotweed with them.

Round and round they flew, tying her up with the vines.

"Stop that!" Lady Nightshade shrieked, waving her arms this way and that.

"Keep going!" Poppy called to Rose and Ninad, and they flew faster and faster as Lady Nightshade tried to wriggle free.

"You'd better stop or you'll be sorry!" Lady Nightshade yelled.

"You'll be sorry," Rose puffed as she flew around Lady Nightshade's arms, tying them up in knotweed.

The fairies didn't stop until Lady

Nightshade was completely in knots
and unable to move.

"That should stop her from spreading
that horrid leaf mould!" Poppy said.

"Let's help Mrs Fluffytail and the
other red pandas," Ninad said.

While they were tying up Lady
Nightshade, the red pandas had come
out of the forest. They started to gather
as many seeds as they could from the
bamboo flowers.

Poppy, Ninad and Rose joined in,
flying to reach the higher flowers.
They used the air magic spell that
Ms Mayblossom had taught them to

gather the seeds and place them into straw baskets.

Soon, the baskets were overflowing with seeds.

Poppy turned to check on Lady Nightshade and froze in fear.

"She's escaping!" she gasped.

Webby was chomping his way through the knotweed and Lady Nightshade had managed to break free. She flew into the air and aimed her toadstool at the leaf mould with an evil cackle.

Chapter Seven

"No!" Poppy yelled. "I won't let you hurt this forest any more!"

She flew into the air and raced over to Lady Nightshade. While Lady Nightshade used her toadstool to spread the leaf mould, Poppy pointed her wand at the mould, trying to suck it back again.

"Pluck and pull, drag and haul, yank

them all!" Poppy cried, over and over
again.

Lady Nightshade glanced at Poppy
and grinned. "You're no match for me,
you pesky little fairy," she hissed.

She aimed her toadstool at the
leaf mould but to

Poppy's surprise, the mould didn't budge. It hung in the air between them as they both tried to use their magic to move it. It was like a tug of war as the leaf mould floated a little way to Lady Nightshade, then a little way back to Poppy. Poppy fought as hard as she could, keeping her magic focused on the leaf mould.

"You can do it, Poppy!" Rose shouted from below.

"Yes, come on, Poppy!" Ninad cried.

That gave Poppy the extra boost she needed. She tugged back at the leaf mould and it started to move slowly in her direction and away from the grip of Lady Nightshade.

Down below, Ninad had rounded up the red pandas. They raced over to chase away Webby and Lady Nightshade, throwing sticks of bamboo at them.

Lady Nightshade shrieked in anger and lowered her toadstool as the red pandas continued to pelt her.

"This isn't over, Poppy Merrymoss!"
she yelled, before fleeing with Webby
on her head.

Poppy fell to the ground, exhausted.

Ninad, Rose and the red pandas ran
over to her.

"That was awesome!" Ninad exclaimed.

"I can't believe you beat Lady Nightshade!" Rose said, giving Poppy a big hug.

Poppy sat up slowly and smiled at them gratefully. "With the help of you two and the red pandas." She shook her head as she watched Lady Nightshade fly off into the distance, still yelling and screaming as the pandas continued to throw bamboo sticks at her. *How had she managed to beat Lady Nightshade? Surely her magic was much more powerful than Poppy's?*

She shuddered as a horrible thought came to her. *I hope I'm not a fungus fairy too!*

They helped the red pandas gather the last of the bamboo seeds. Poppy flew up to a bright red flower. As she reached in to pull out the seeds, she froze. Inside was a beautiful magic seed. It was striped red and black, just like a red panda's tail.

She carefully picked up the seed and flew down to her friends.

"Look what I've found!" she cried.

"Another magic seed!" Rose squealed. "That'll show that evil Lady Nightshade!

"We should take it back to your aunt," Ninad said.

Poppy tucked the seed into the front pocket of her overalls and looked around the bamboo forest.

"There is still so much knotweed," she said.

"And dead bamboo," Mrs Fluffytail sighed.

"We'll help clear it up," Rose told her.

They quickly got to work using the air spell they were taught to pull up the knotweed and clear the dead bamboo into piles. When it was all clear, they planted the bamboo seeds.

Mrs Fluffytail stared at the ground sadly. "Bamboo does grow very quickly, but I'm not sure this bamboo will grow in time to save us," she said.

Poppy noticed that Rose had a

mischievous glint in her eye.

"What if we used Lady Nightshade's extra powerful leaf mould to do some good?" she suggested.

"You're brilliant, Rose!" Poppy said, hugging her friend. "If we use just a little of the leaf mould, the bamboo will grow in no time," she explained to Mrs Fluffytail.

"And you won't have to go hungry," Ninad added.

They sprinkled a small amount of leaf mould on the bamboo seeds and waited to see if their plan had worked.

While they waited, Poppy, Rose and

Ninad played with Tear and his baby brother and sisters. Ninad and Rose built them a climbing frame using some of the old bamboo. The red pandas clambered over it happily, giggling and cheering as they hung upside down.

Finally, the new bamboo grew to its full height. Poppy was glad to see there were no more flowers.

"We have to get back to school," she told the red pandas.

Tear gave each of the fairies a big hug in turn, and Poppy thought she saw real tears sliding down his face.

"We'll come back to visit you whenever we can," Ninad promised.

Mrs Fluffytail stepped forward, holding out three garlands made from bamboo flowers.

"I made these for you," she said as she placed one over each of the fairies' heads. "To say thank you for all you've done to help us."

"Thank you!" the fairies chorused.

Poppy looked at her friends. "Let's get this magic seed back to Oakwings," she said.

She patted Tear, wiping away a tear of her own, and they waved goodbye to their new red panda friends and flew off towards home.

Chapter Eight

They flew as fast as they could, past the Whispering Waterfall and the mountains, until they were back in their own forest.

Most of the knotweed had been cleared away, to Poppy's relief.

"We should take this to Aunt Lily," Poppy said as she headed towards the greenhouses where she knew she would find Ms Mayblossom.

But as they turned the corner, they almost bumped into Ms Webcap, who was charging the other way. She crossed her arms and glared at them.

Rose started to giggle and nudged Poppy with her elbow. She pointed at Ms Webcap's head. A piece of knotweed was caught in her hair.

"I wonder how that got there?" Poppy said, with a knowing grin.

Ms Webcap grabbed at the knotweed and yanked it out, dropping it on to the floor in disgust.

"Thanks for helping us grow a new

bamboo forest for the red pandas," Poppy continued.

Although he looked terrified of Ms Webcap, Ninad couldn't help a little smirk of his own. "We would never have been able to do it without your special leaf mould," he said.

"Or got this magic seed," Poppy added, patting the seed in her pocket.

Ms Webcap began to shake with anger and her face blazed red. She took a step towards the friends and held out her toadstool. On her head, Webby had woken. His eyes glinted as he watched them hungrily.

Ninad took a step back, but Poppy
and Rose stood their ground. Poppy
glared right back at Ms Webcap.

"Is everything all right?" a sing-song voice called out behind them.

Poppy had never been so happy to see her aunt before. Ms Mayblossom joined Poppy, looking at Ms Webcap in concern.

"Everything is fine," Ms Webcap hissed through gritted teeth. She swung her cloak over her shoulder and hurried off.

"That's strange," Ms Mayblossom said as she watched Ms Webcap go. "I could have sworn I saw Ms Webcap's hat move just then!"

Poppy smiled slyly at Ninad and

Rose. *Maybe one day Ms Webcap will show her true colours,* she thought, *and the teachers will finally realise that she is Lady Nightshade.*

She dug around in her pocket and pulled out the stripy magic seed. "Look what we found!"

Ms Mayblossom gasped as she took the seed from Poppy. She stared at it in wonder. "I've never seen a seed quite like this," she said. "Wherever did you find it?"

They told her about finding Tear, the little red panda, and the riddle of finding out where he came from and

what he was trying to tell them. When
Ms Mayblossom heard about how they
had helped to gather the bamboo seeds
and plant and grow a new bamboo
forest, she looked like she might burst
with pride. She hugged each of them in
turn.

"I am so proud of you all!" Ms
Mayblossom said.

Ninad blushed and looked
at the ground,
while Rose
hugged Poppy.

"Poppy was amazing!" Rose said. "You should have seen how she managed to fight against Lady Nightshade's magic to get the leaf mould."

Aunt Lily smiled. "I'm glad you managed to save the red pandas' forest," she said. "But you must be careful when it comes to Lady Nightshade."

Poppy nodded quickly, then changed the subject. She didn't want to think about how her magic seemed to be evenly matched with Lady Nightshade's. There was no way Poppy

ever wanted to become a fungus fairy!

"I wished there was something we could do with all of the dead bamboo," she said wistfully.

Ms Mayblossom smiled. "Oh, don't worry about that," she said. "There's plenty we can do. Nothing in the forest goes to waste."

The next day at breakfast, Madame Brightglow had an announcement. She looked much brighter than she had a few days ago. Sunbeams seemed to burst out of her when she smiled.

"All classes are cancelled for today,"
she told them. "To say thank you to all
of you for such hard work clearing our
forest of knotweed, we are taking you
on a special mystery outing!"

The Great Hall exploded with cheers
of excitement.

Rose's eyes were wide. "Where do you think we are going?" she asked.

"Maybe sledding at the Magic Mountains?" Ninad suggested.

"Or swimming in Little Boat Bay," said Poppy.

They soon found out. As they flew through the forest to their destination, Poppy realised that the path seemed familiar.

"Is that the Whispering Waterfall?" she asked.

"And the mountains?" Rose said.

Ninad's eyes lit up. "We're going to the bamboo forest!" he cried.

Mrs Fluffytail, Tear and the baby red pandas greeted them as they arrived, then Ms Mayblossom called their class over to a patch of the forest where the red pandas had piled up the dead bamboo.

"Nothing goes to waste in the forest," she told the class. "Just as we can use dead leaves for mulch to help the plants and flowers grow, we can use this old bamboo."

She showed them how to make things using the bamboo, just like how Ninad and Rose had built a climbing frame for the baby pandas.

Poppy and Rose made cups and
straws and Celeste made some bracelets,
which Poppy had to admit were
actually quite nice. Ms Mayblossom
helped Ninad make a small slide for
the red pandas to play on.

At lunchtime, she brought around fresh elderberry juice, which Rose and Poppy drank using their bamboo cups and straws. Everyone though their idea was so good that they all made their own cups and straws too.

Celeste held up her cup for everyone to admire. "I think *my* cup is definitely the best," she boasted. "It's even got a little handle, look!"

She was so loud that she frightened one of the baby red pandas. He hid beneath Celeste's skirt, and while she was screaming and spinning around trying to get him out, Poppy noticed something.

She nudged Rose with her elbow. "Do you smell that?" she asked.

Rose burst into giggles, while Ninad ran to help rescue the baby red panda.

"Oh!" Celeste shrieked. "It stinks!"

"He's only making that smell because you're scaring him!" Ninad said.

"Are you sure that's not your perfume?" Rose called out.

Ninad finally managed to coax the baby panda away from Celeste and he clung to Ninad as Celeste ran away, holding her nose.

Poppy and Rose laughed so much that tears ran down their faces.

When they had calmed down, Poppy sighed. "I'm so pleased we solved the riddle of the red panda," she said, watching Tear and the babies play on their new climbing frame and slide.

"Me too," Rose agreed.

"Who would have guessed that Lady Nightshade would end up accidentally helping us too!" Ninad said.

Poppy nodded. "She may have helped us accidentally, but she nearly destroyed the red pandas' bamboo forest. Who knows what she might be planning next!" She gave her friends a determined smile. "But as long as we work together, we know we'll be able to beat her."

The End

Have you read the other books in the series?

Fairy Forest School

Poppy Merrymoss and her best friends, Ninad Cleardrop and Rose Seedpip, are taking part in the Starlight Dance Show. But before their big performane, Lady Nightshade puts a curse on the forest, making it night time for ever! Can the friends reverse the spell in time for the big show?

Find out what happens in:

Starlight Adventure